Nobody knows for sure when golems were first thought of, but they've been around in Jewish culture for thousands of years. Back then, a golem was a half-formed creature – a kind of spirit.

Later on, in the Middle Ages, people became very interested in magic and they tried to make persons from clay or wood. Legend tells us they called these images golems. The usual way to make one was to write the word truth on a slip of paper and put it in the mouth or on the forehead of the image while a secret formula was said.

The golem stories grew very popular in the 16th century, when the world grew even more dangerous than usual for Jewish people. The golems became their protectors.

The most famous golem was made by Rabbi Judah Low of Prague, in the 1500s. And from that time, every generation had a favourite golem to help in time of need. In most legends the golem can't speak, he simply obeys. But before we knew it, our golem had a voice and a mind of his own. And we really like him that way.

ANNA and BARBARA FIENBERG

ANNA and BARBARA FIENBERG write the Tashi stories together, making up all kinds of daredevil adventures and tricky characters for him to face. Lucky he's such a clever Tashi.

KIM GAMBLE is one of Australia's favourite illustrators for children. Together Kim and Anna have made such wonderful books as *The Magnificent Nose and Other Marvels*, *The Hottest Boy Who Ever Lived*, the *Tashi* series, the *Minton* picture books, *Joseph*, *There once was a boy called Tashi*, and *The Amazing Tashi Activity Book*.

First published in 2009

Allen & Unwin
83 Alexander Street
Crows Nest 2065
Australia
Phone: (61 2) 8425 0100
Fax: (61 2) 9906 2218
Email: info@allenandunwin.com
Web: www.allenandunwin.com

Cataloguing-in-Publication details are available
from the National Library of Australia
www.trove.nla.gov.au

ISBN 978 1 74175 792 7

The text pages of this book are printed on:
• paper [made/derived] from forests promoting sustainable forest management.
• Australian-made ENVI Carbon Neutral paper. ENVI is certified
  by the Australian Government.

Cover and series design by Sandra Nobes
Typeset in Sabon by Tou-Can Design
This book was printed in September 2011 at McPherson's Printing Group,
76 Nelson St, Maryborough, Victoria 3465, Australia.
www.mcphersonsprinting.com.au

10 9 8 7 6

www.tashibooks.com

Tashi

and the
GOLEM

written by
Anna Fienberg
and
Barbara Fienberg

illustrated by
Kim Gamble

ALLEN&UNWIN

'Anybody sitting here?' Frank Fury squashed
down between Jack and Tashi. He peered
into Tashi's lunchbox. '*Erk*, what d'you call
that?' And he stuck a big dirty finger right
into the middle of a sandwich.

'Dragon egg,' said Jack, helping himself
to one. 'And get your paws off it.'

'Who's gunna make me?' said Frank,
and shoved Jack just under his ribs so that
he dropped his sandwich on the ground.

'Hey, look out, you *dill* blot!' cried Jack.

'*You* look out, dog breath,' Frank held
up his fists, 'or you could hurt yourself
on *these*.'

Tashi finished his sandwich and gazed
at Frank's fists. 'Strong hands. Good for
working in the fields, or digging a well. Big
Uncle could have done with hands like yours
when we were digging for treasure.'

'What? Who's Big Uncle?' Frank's voice
was gruff but a small smile pricked at the
corner of his mouth. He laid his left hand,
fingers splayed wide, on his knee for
everyone to see.

2

'Now *that's* a story you'll never hear,'
said Jack, 'because you can't even appreciate
dragon eggs.'

Frank went red. He leapt up and loomed
over Jack, his fists up.

'Not many people in the world have heard
of dragon eggs,' Tashi went on. 'Let alone
tasted one. It's a shame because they're
delicious. My friend Ah Chu likes them even
better than giants' dumplings.'

Frank stared at Tashi, confused. He
looked at his fists hovering in the air, as if
he didn't know what they were doing there.
Then he shook his head in a scornful way,
and stumped off.

'What a loser,' muttered Jack. 'He's only been here a day and already everyone hates him. I bet he'll thump someone and kill them and then he'll have to go to *jail*.'

'Hmm,' said Tashi. 'People do change, though. You can't be sure what they're going to do next. It's like the weather. Something could happen in between today's rain and tomorrow. The sun might come out!' Tashi gazed off into the distance.

'Are you talking about someone in particular?'

'Well, I'm thinking of Bang Bang, right now. But a minute ago I was thinking of Soh Sorry, Soh Meen's son.'

'So start with Bang Bang, who was he?'

'Someone you might say would end up in jail.' Tashi took a bite of his apple. 'Bang Bang rubbed everyone up the wrong way. Including me. But Ah Chu was the first to come up against him.'

'What happened?'

'Well, it was like this. One day Lotus Blossom and I were walking to school and we met Ah Chu. He was kicking along his bag, instead of carrying it, and muttering some really bad words. I was amazed because the bag was very special to him, and inside there might be dumplings or fish cakes getting all bashed up.

'As soon as he saw us he growled, "Did you know the Baron's nephew, Bang Bang, has come to stay with him?"

'"What's he like?" I asked.

'"What would you ex*pect* a nephew of the Baron to be like?" said Ah Chu.

'"Oh, greedy," Lotus Blossom shrugged, "a bit of a bully, just like his uncle?"

'"Not necessarily," I said. "Look at Soh Meen's son, who isn't mean at all, but tries extra hard to make up for his father. My grandma says it is a terrible burden for a young man to carry and that's why Soh Sorry went away. You have to see someone for who they are, not where they've come from."

'"That's all very well," Ah Chu cut in, "but Lotus Blossom is right about Bang Bang. I met him while I was unwrapping a sticky rice cake that your mother had given me, Tashi, when he grabbed it and ate it and tipped me upside down to see if I had any more in my pockets. Then he said he'd beat me with his bamboo cane if I told anyone."

'"What a pig!" This is just the sort of thing that makes Lotus Blossom boil. "I hope he doesn't stay long."

'That afternoon I saw Bang Bang for myself. He was swaggering through the village as if he owned it. When my Auntie Tam didn't move out of his way quickly enough, he pushed her so roughly she fell into a basket of beans waiting ready for market.

'I helped her to her feet and said to Bang Bang, "Look what you're doing. You could have hurt her!"

'Bang Bang grabbed my arm and twisted it up behind my back until the pain took my breath away. Then he spun me around and, poking me in the chest with each word, hissed, "I've heard about you, young Tashi. You stay out of my way or we'll be having these arm exercises every day." He lifted me up so that his face was right in mine. "Did you hear me?"

'I nodded and he dropped me, *flop*, on the ground. Then he strolled away, well pleased with himself.

'I stood still till my heart stopped hammering. No one had behaved like that to me before. As if I was a bag of old fish heads. Even the Baron treated me like a respected enemy. I could see why people were frightened of Bang Bang. It was as if he didn't understand other people had feelings at all.

'I was still sore and troubled the next day when we bumped into Much-to-Learn coming out of Not Yet's shop. He was bursting with news and rage. But it wasn't because his shoes weren't ready.'

'No, it was that bully Bang Bang, wasn't it?' Jack burst out. 'What's he done *now*?'

'Well,' said Tashi, 'Much-to-Learn said Bang Bang had called around, saying that he and the Baron had decided the spring bubbling up at the back of Wise-as-an-Owl's house really belonged to the Baron. "We own the field next door and we say that fence was put in the wrong place. The spring is on the Baron's land, and we are going to take it over."

'"He can't do that!" I shouted. "Your father uses that special spring water for his medicines. Besides, it has belonged to his family for hundreds of years."

'"Yes, but my father just won't take him seriously," Much-to-Learn fretted. "Really, I think Bang Bang is a very dangerous young man. I'm afraid that he and the Baron will just march in and take over the spring."

'That's just the kind of thing Frank Fury would do,' said Jack. 'If he wants something he'll get it, and look out anybody who's in his way.'

'Well, so you can imagine how we felt. Something had to be done quickly. We were standing in the square, thinking, when Much-to-Learn said nervously, "I learned a new spell the other day, Tashi, that might just be useful."

'Lotus Blossom caught my eye and shook her head. I knew she was thinking about how Much-to-Learn's last spell, the mixed-up monster, had turned out. But he was so much more careful these days. I didn't think he'd make a mistake like that again.

'So I listened closely while he explained that he had been reading in the Book of Spells about a little creature called a golem. "You make it from clay and then, when you chant a spell, you can bring it to life."

'"*Wah!* Have you actually done it, Much-to-Learn?" we wanted to know.

'"No. Not actually *done* it, not yet, but–" Much-to-Learn took my arm and led me a few steps away to the gloomy lane behind Not Yet's shop. In a whisper, he repeated the spell three or four times until I knew it by heart.

'"That's it!" I cried when we came back to the others. "Only we won't make a little golem, we'll shape a great big one!"

'Much-to-Learn looked still more anxious when he heard this and seemed sorry he'd ever mentioned the spell. Even Lotus Blossom said, "And then what? What happens when it comes to life?"

'But Ah Chu was excited. "If you bring it to life, it would have to be your servant, wouldn't it?"

'I wasn't so sure, but if Wise-as-an-Owl wouldn't see the danger we were facing, it seemed the best thing to do. So we told Much-to-Learn not to worry, we would be careful, that he should go back and keep Wise-as-an-Owl occupied.

'Then we ran home, collected our buckets
and met at the river bank. All afternoon
we trundled loads of mud up to a grassy
clearing and when we had a really huge pile,
we began to shape the Golem.

'Pale pink was seeping into the sky when we sat back and looked at what we had done. A cool breeze suddenly sprang up, and as I gazed at the Golem lying in the grass, I wasn't sure if it was the sudden chill in the air or my own uneasiness that lifted the hair on my neck.

'The Golem was about three metres long, with arms and legs like trunks and a huge block of a head.

'Lotus Blossom shivered. "I don't like the look on his face." She smoothed over the grim mouth and turned up the lips in a smile.

'"That's better," I said. "He looks friendlier now. And just to make sure, we'll give him a heart. There's a pine cone behind you, Ah Chu."

'I took from my pocket a piece of paper with the sacred word *LIFE* written on it and put it under the Golem's tongue, and then, with a fine stick wrote the word once more on his forehead.

'"We have to light three fires now: one at the head and two at the feet, using cedar branches," I told them. I was getting nervous again. It was all very well for Lotus Blossom and Ah Chu – they hadn't heard the incantation, so haunting and mysterious in the shadows of that lane. They didn't know how Much-to-Learn had tried to keep his voice hushed and low on the ground, but even so the spell had tugged at the air and risen up with a life of its own, flickering between us.

'Yet as we went about lighting the sticks, I felt a little shudder of excitement, too, thinking of how Bang Bang might change from a swaggering bully to a – a what? What would he do when he saw the Golem?

'We each stood by a fire and I lifted my voice, repeating the chant I had learned. And with every word the sun slipped further into the river, and the long shadows of the willows rippled out from the bank. And as I spoke, the scented smoke thickened and danced around the Golem.

'The breeze dropped as we waited, and the river was still. We watched the drifting smoke and the hulking clay figure hidden inside it and it seemed the whole world was holding its breath with us. Slowly, through the haze, we saw two lights shining. We stood transfixed: the Golem had opened his eyes.

'A tremor passed over the huge body and the giant sat up. Lotus Blossom gasped. Ah Chu sank to his knees.

'The Golem turned his great head. "Who are you?" His voice was rough, like grinding gravel.

'I quickly explained what we had done, and why.

'The giant frowned. "The Golem does no man's bidding."

'Ah Chu found his voice. "Oh, but you must. We brought you to life, so that makes you our servant … doesn't it?" His question dribbled away to a squeak.

'The Golem surged to his feet and towered above us. He was tall as a ship. "I am hungry," he said. He plucked Ah Chu up and sniffed his arm, hastily dropping him back.

'"What do I like to eat?" He looked at us reproachfully. "You have given me a heart but no memory."

'We offered him some nettles and a dead lizard but he didn't like them. Then Ah Chu remembered the fish balls and the honey cakes in his bag. Sadly, he watched the Golem devour them. "What golems like are fish balls and honey cakes," Ah Chu sighed.

'There was a sudden loud gurgle from the Golem's stomach and a gulp from his mouth. "What was that?" he asked, surprised.

'"That was a burp," Ah Chu told him. "It's because you ate too quickly. The wind comes up and out your mouth."

'The Golem did it again. "I can taste the food I just ate," he said wonderingly.

'"That's right!" Ah Chu cried excitedly. "It happens to me all the time." He stood beaming at the Golem until he noticed we were grinning at him.

'"We could bring you some more food tomorrow if you will just give a *certain person* a good scare," I told him.

'"The certain person is called Bang Bang," added Ah Chu, just in case.

'"I'll think about it," the Golem replied. "But now I have a strong feeling that it is time for me to have a little rest. This living business is very tiring for a golem." And he lay back down, *whumpff*, on the flattened bushes to sleep.

'"We gave him a lovely smile," said Lotus Blossom with satisfaction.

'"And he has a noble forehead," said Ah Chu gruffly.

'The Golem opened one eye, "And good burps." We waited. "So, this Bang Bang you were talking about," he went on, "what do you want me to do to him? Tear him apart?"

'"No!" I shouted.

'"Throw him across the river?"

'"No, no!" Lotus Blossom went white.

'"Stand on him?" We shook our heads. "*Lean* on him?" His eyes twinkled. I could swear that he was enjoying himself.

'We walked home very quietly, I can tell
you. There was just a sliver of moon and
the dark hung between the trees like a
curtain. We jumped at the sudden hoot of
an owl. "Yesterday I didn't think we would
be worried about looking after Bang Bang,
did you?" whispered Lotus Blossom as we
reached the empty square. Before parting we
agreed on the food we would bring to the
Golem, and then we each made the sign of
the dragon, for luck.

'The next afternoon after school we arrived at the river bank, but there was no Golem. We ran along the bend of the river, searching, and then into the forest, and we were wishing we had never heard of golems and wondering what harm such a creature would do in the village when we heard heavy steps and snapped branches coming towards us.

'But it wasn't the Golem. It was Bang Bang.

'"Hah!" he cried. "Tashi and his little friends! I'm on my way to tell our men where to put the new fence. I'm going to –" but he noticed that we weren't looking at him any longer. We were staring over his shoulder at something else.

'The Golem had been lying among the bushes right behind Bang Bang and now he sat up. Bang Bang turned and gasped. He looked back at us in terror as the Golem slowly rose to his feet.

'"Is this the Bang Bang you were talking about?" the Golem asked.

'I nodded and went over to him, reaching up to take his hand. "This is our friend, the Golem," I told Bang Bang. "And you are – what? Our enemy? Friend?"

'"Oh friend, your *friend*," stammered Bang Bang and he searched frantically in his pockets, finally pulling out a piece of bamboo shoot. "Here," he said, offering it to the Golem as if he were a savage dog. The Golem took the bamboo, cautiously nibbling an end of it. A pleased smile spread across his face.

'"*This* is what Golems like!" he said.

'"It came from across those mountains," Bang Bang told him eagerly. "Not far from where I grew up. I could draw a map to show you where." He pulled out some paper and a pencil from another pocket but after a few minutes the Golem said impatiently, "I can't read those squiggles. You'll have to come with me and show me the way."

'Bang Bang looked stunned. "On second thoughts, it's a rather lonely forest where those shoots grow, a long way from any village or people."

'"Good," said the Golem, "that's just what I like – not all this talking, talking, talking, just the wind in the trees and the birds singing." He looked around, surprised and pleased. "That's what I *like*!"

'"But first we'd have to get some food for the journey," Bang Bang pointed out anxiously.

'"Here you are," we all cried together, holding out the food that we'd brought for the Golem.

'"Fish balls," beamed Ah Chu.

'"Honey cakes," I cried.

'"And plenty of carrots," Lotus Blossom added.

'Bang Bang glared at us but he couldn't think of any more objections. The Golem bent and scooped him up under his arm. He gave us a little smile and a wave as he strode off along the path. "Tell my uncle–" Bang Bang began but the rest was lost as they passed into the forest.

'Much-to-Learn was overjoyed to hear the news of what had happened. He hadn't had a moment's peace since he'd taught me the spell, he said, and he would rather we didn't mention it to anyone else.

'A few days later I heard the Baron talking to Luk Ahed in the village. "Young people today have no manners. That nephew of mine was supposed to be making a long visit with me but he just took himself off without a word of thanks or goodbye. I had a letter from his father this morning saying that he doesn't know what I did with him, but he's a different boy, obedient and polite and helpful to his mother. He can't get over it, but you can be sure I won't be asking Bang Bang to come and stay with me again!"

'I wish *we* had a Golem,' said Jack, watching Frank snatch Angus Figment's tennis ball and put it in his pocket.

'What you looking at?' said Frank, as he swaggered past.

'A Bang Bang in need of a golem,' said Jack.

'What? You guys talk rubbish.'

'You'd understand if you'd heard Tashi's story. Could be the story of your life,' said Jack.

'Oh yeah?' Frank held up his fists. 'Well these could be the end of yours!'

'Bang Bang had a brother, you know,'
Tashi said. 'But that's another story.'

'Yeah?' said Frank. 'How does that one go?'

'Well,' said Tashi, 'it was like this.'

'Like what?'

'Oh, let him get on with it,' said Jack.
'He always starts this way.'

'Can I have my ball back, Frank?' Angus
Figment crept up, looking down at his shoes.
'If you're quite finished with it?'

Everyone looked at Frank.

'If you give the ball back,' said Tashi, 'then
I can start the story.'

'Tell me what's in it then,' said Frank.
'And I'll see.'

'Oh, kidnappings and river pirates...'

'Okay, here's your ball, Figment. It was a
dumb ball anyway.'

'Oh, thanks so much!' said Angus, and he
sat down on the bench.

'So, okay, *start* then,' said Frank. He
smirked. 'Anybody sitting here?'

'Yes *I* am,' said Jack. 'Can't you see? Find
your own seat for once.'

'Well, it was like this...' Tashi began.

THINKS-TOO-LATE

'Remember, Jack, how disgusted the Baron
was with the rude way his nephew Bang
Bang left him?'

'Who's this Bang Bang?' Frank interrupted.

'A rude guy, a bully just like you,' said
Jack.

'Hey, who are you calling a –'

'Shut up, Frank, you might learn
something,' said Angus suddenly. Everyone
stopped talking and looked at him.
He smiled, 'That's if you don't mind.'

'Well,' Tashi went on, 'as Jack explained, Bang Bang was a bully, and he'd made everyone's life a misery, so you can imagine how surprised they were in the village to hear about the Baron's next visitor. It was Bang Bang's young brother! Their father had written to say that the Baron had done such a good job with Bang Bang, he was hoping that the Baron might take his other son in hand.'

'Ha, the *Baron* doing a good job, what a joke!' said Jack.

'*What* joke? I'm not laughing,' said Frank.

'Just listen, and you'll get it,' said Angus.

'Well, this younger brother, he was like
a hurricane, stirring up trouble wherever he
went. By the time he was five, his family had
named him Thinks-Too-Late because he was
always doing terrible things without thinking
what the results would be.'

'At least he *did* stuff,' said Frank. 'I mean,
he didn't just sit around on his bum all day
doing *nothing*.'

'Go on, Tashi,' said Angus.

'Well, he certainly looked a completely
different sort of person from Bang Bang.
He was a cheerful, smiling boy, interested
in everyone he met and full of suggestions
for what they should be doing.'

'See?' said Frank, slapping his knee, 'what did I tell you? A helpful guy, handy to have around!'

'On the very first day that he bounced into our village, he persuaded three small boys to jump off the schoolhouse roof to see which one would land first.'

'Yeah,' said Jack, 'such a *help*ful guy!'

'Then he talked Little Wu into seeing if you could spark a fire by striking a piece of metal on a brick. You can, and it was just luck that Not Yet's storeroom didn't go up in flames before he found out what they were doing.

'Thinks-Too-Late couldn't see what all the fuss was about, and soon he turned his attention to the problem of Granny White Eyes. Everyone had been worried about her since Mrs Ping had found her dazed and sore after a fall in her kitchen. It wasn't the first time this had happened, and now lots of people wanted her to go and live with them.

'But Granny White Eyes wouldn't even think about it. "I can manage perfectly well on my own. It's what I like and I would miss my own little house and my garden too much."

'Thinks-Too-Late didn't take part in these discussions, but later he caught my arm. "I know how we can convince her that she can't live alone anymore. We can give her frights. No, listen, it'll be interesting – and it's for her own good."

'I heard him out in silence. He suggested we could pretend to be burglars and ghosts and make phantom door knocks at her cottage in the evenings. Lotus Blossom, who had come up in time to hear this, was speechless for once, but I couldn't help angry words exploding out of me.

'"Listen you, if you so much as go *near* Granny White Eyes, we will see that no one in the village speaks to you again."

'But Thinks-Too-Late didn't mind.
"Okay," he said cheerfully, and with a breezy
wave of his hand, he set off to call on Wise-
as-an-Owl. He sneaked around the house
to the back window and listened as Wise-
as-an-Owl was listing for Much-to-Learn
the ingredients of a new medicine they
were mixing.

'The next thing they knew, poor Mrs Yang was covered in huge purple and red blotches. "That awful boy told me it was Wise-as-an-Owl's new cure for backache!" she moaned.

'But Thinks-too-Late didn't mind being scolded. Particularly when he heard Soh Meen loudly complaining around the village about how bad his cold was. "I know what you need!" he cried, and ran off to fetch a capful of dark green plants.

'"What have you got there?" asked Soh Meen suspiciously. He was even more doubtful when he saw Thinks-Too-Late take off his socks and pull them over his hands before picking up the plants.

'"This is just what you need," beamed Thinks-Too-Late. "Open your shirt." He rubbed the plants vigorously into Soh Meen's chest.

'The next moment Soh Meen was running around in circles, tearing off his shirt. "I'm stinging and burning and stinging!" he cried. "Those were nettles you rubbed into me!"

'"Yes, but haven't they made you lovely and warm?"

'"I said I *had* a cold, you stupid boy, I didn't say I *was* cold! Oh, my skin feels like it's on fire!"

'"Anyway, it's taking his mind off his cold." Thinks-Too-Late winked at me.

'By now everyone in the village had heard about the trouble Thinks-Too-Late had caused. Even so, no one was prepared for what he did next.

'What?' said Frank. 'What did he do?'

'Well, it was like this. One day Lotus Blossom and I called on Ah Chu to ask him to come down to the river for a swim, and to see the River Pirate's new sampan. I'd spotted him that morning pulling in for supplies. Ah Chu said he couldn't go because he had to mind his baby sister. But as we moved on down the road, Ah Chu came running after us. "On second thoughts, Little Sister can come with us. She is eight months old after all – it's time she had her first swim."

'We took turns carrying Little Sister, babies can be quite heavy after a while. We were watching her splash her hands and feet in a shallow pool by the river when Thinks-Too-Late came along.

'Little Sister smiled sweetly at him and offered him a wet bun. It was so pleasant there, talking and joking and rolling in the cool water and out again, the time passed quickly. Until Ah Chu looked around. "Where is Little Sister?" Dread clanged in the air.

'"And where is Thinks-Too-Late?" I cried.

'Ah Chu, his face as white as flour, dived and dived, searching the river. Lotus Blossom and I raced up and down the river bank, calling. It seemed hours before we caught sight of Thinks-Too-Late sneaking back to the village through the trees.

'When we caught up with him, he stammered, "Oh, L-L-Little Sister? I gave her to the River Pirate."

'"You did *what*? What were you thinking of? Can't you imagine how Little Sister's parents will feel? And that little baby without her mother?"

'Thinks-Too-Late shrugged. "I didn't think, and anyway, I had to give her away. See, I took her down to the sampan to show her what a boat was like and the River Pirate saw her. He and his wife don't have any children, and he said his wife told him not to come back without a baby this trip. So he gave me this jade horse to keep me quiet until they'd got away. He said he'd cut me into little pieces with that great sword of his if I told."

'I didn't stop to hear any more of his sniffs and excuses. I grabbed the horse and shouted at him, "*Run!* Run faster than the wind and bring Little Sister's mother down to the boat." Then, "Come on!" I told Lotus Blossom and Ah Chu, and we raced down the path to the landing stage, just in time to see the pirates casting off the ropes from the dock. We leapt onto the boat and swarmed over the pirates, tripping them up, re-tying the ropes, ducking and dodging the big tattooed arms flung out to catch us.

'"Captain Drednort!" we called. "Come out!"

'"What do yer want, fish-bait?" growled the
River Pirate, coming up on deck. When we
told him there had been a terrible mistake and
he had to give the baby back, he just laughed.
But he didn't sound amused. He sounded
angry. His face closed over like a big iron trap.
"A deal is a deal," he snarled. "Pirate's code.
Now get off my boat or I'll chop you up like
sardines and feed you to the sharks."

'Ah Chu let out a moan. He was watching
Little Sister struggling against the shoulder
of a big hairy sailor. "But you can't, you
don't even know—"

'The River Pirate drew out his sword.
It flashed silver fire in the midday sun.
We couldn't stop looking at it, even though
it hurt our eyes. Ah Chu started to weep.
Oh, what to do? And then, out of the corner
of my eye, I saw something. Someone was
flashing past the stacks of lumber, leaping
over coils of rope, *flying* along... Thinks-
too-Late racing to reach us! And on his heels,
Ah Chu's mother! As she spotted us she took
a heart-stopping leap and sprang on board,
holding her arms out for her child.

'Little Sister wanted her mother. She began to wail.

'"Listen to that," I said quickly. "How will you and your men enjoy the trip home with that baby screaming in your ears all day?" His men looked very impressed with this argument, but the River Pirate just shrugged and said a good smack would keep him quiet.

'"Him?" said Mrs Chu, grabbing her child, "Little Sister is not a *him*."

'"It's not?" bellowed the River Pirate. "Do you mean to say I have bought a girl?"

'Lotus Blossom's chin jutted out, like it always does when she's in a temper. "What's wrong with being a girl? We're just as good as boys any day."

'The River Pirate brushed her aside and turned to Mrs Chu. "As well as returning my jade horse," he said as he lifted it from my hands, "I will need some compensation from you for my trouble."

'Poor Mrs Chu looked at me in despair. She had no money or jewels to give the River Pirate. None of us did. And wasn't that the only thing that would satisfy him? But as I watched her wringing her hands, an idea popped into my mind. There was no time to look at it from all sides as I usually do. It just had to work, and it was the truth.

'"You will need to go and ask the Baron then," I said to the River Pirate, "seeing that it was the Baron's nephew, Thinks-Too-Late, who sold the baby to you."

'A strange smile broke out on the River Pirate's face. "Oh ho, he is, is he?" And the pirate grabbed Thinks-Too-Late by the scruff of his neck. "Then let's go and visit your *uncle*, my little blabbermouth," he spat. "We'll see what he has to say about the way his nephew does business. He'll pay a tidy sum to keep this matter quiet, I think."

'As we watched him march Thinks-Too-Late down the path to the Baron's house, Mrs Chu snuggled Little Sister into her. "When the Baron has to open his money bags, he won't be wanting to keep Thinks-Too-Late with him much longer," she said with satisfaction.

'Lotus Blossom did a little dance. "Granny White Eyes will be pleased."

'And the baby laughed in agreement, sucking her mother's nose.

'Er yuck,' said Frank. 'Babies are disgusting.'

'Is that all you can say?' cried Angus Figment. 'Little Sister nearly got kidnapped forever!'

'Well, would *you* want to suck someone's nose?' said Frank. 'Even for fifty bucks?'

The boys were quiet a moment, considering.

'I dreamed my little sister got kidnapped once,' said Frank. 'It was an amazing dream. It had all the features of a great adventure: pirates, quicksand, bugs living in your ears, sea snakes.'

Everyone stared at Frank.

'Let's hear it!' said Tashi.

'Yeah!' said Jack.

'Maybe tomorrow,' said Frank. He grinned at them all. 'Sometimes it's good sitting round doing nothing, hey?'